Stop that Cow!

Written by Mairi Mackinnon

Illustrated by Fred Blunt

How this book works

The story of **Stop that Cow!** has been written for you to read with your child. You take turns to read:

You read these words.

Lily the silly cow wants to go far.

"This farm is so dull."

"How I long for a big red car."

4

5

Your child reads these words.

You don't have to finish the story in one session. If your child is getting tired, put a marker in the page and come back to it later.

You can find out more about helping your child with this book, and with reading in general, on pages 30-31.

Stop that Cow!

Turn the page to start the story.

Lily the silly cow wants to go far.

"This farm is so dull."

"How I long for
a big red car."

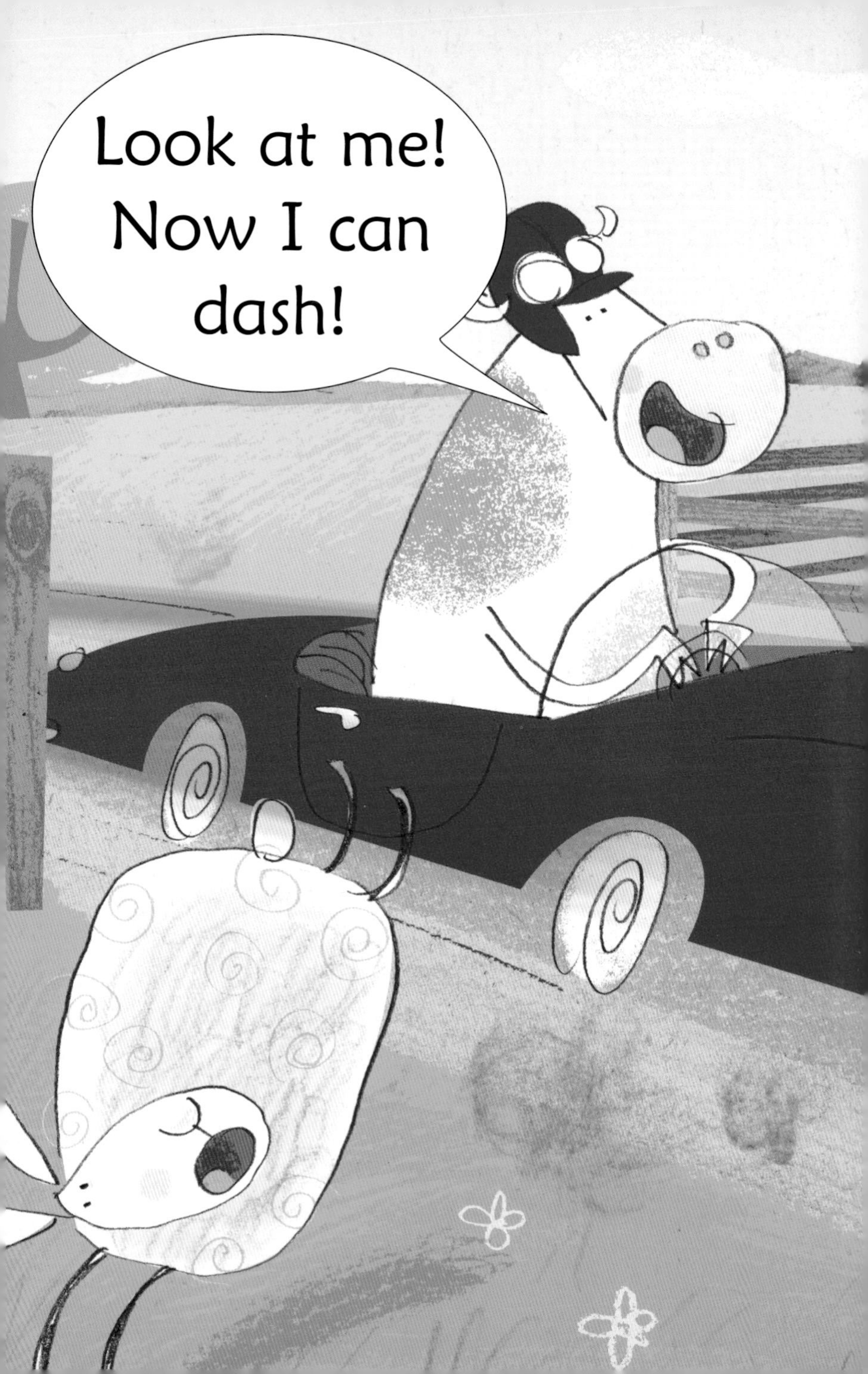
Look at me! Now I can dash!

Beep!
Beep!

7

Now she's Lightning Lil,
and she's going to town.

Near and far,
and up and down.

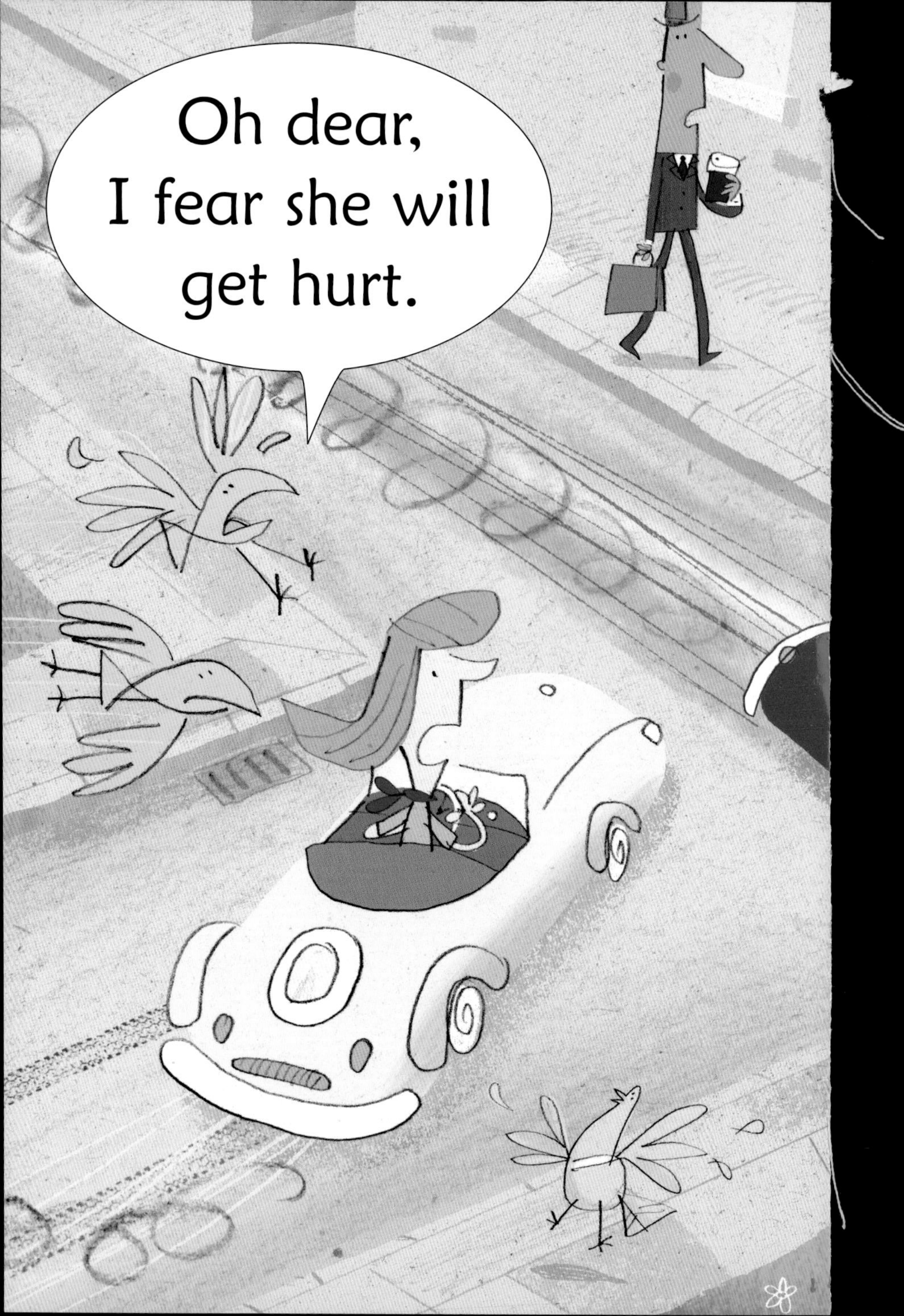
Oh dear, I fear she will get hurt.

11

Lightning Lil is out of control.

13

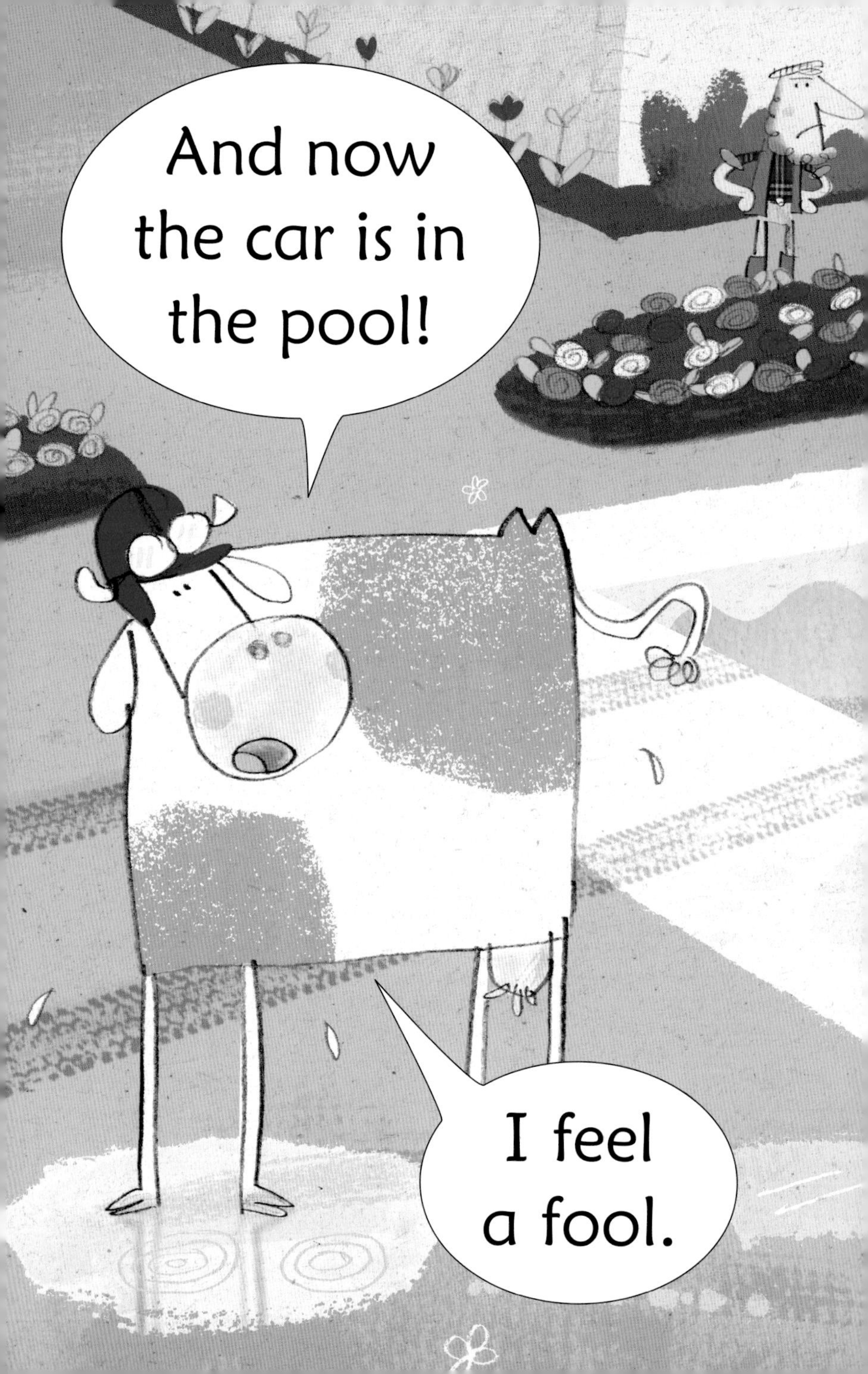
And now the car is in the pool!
I feel a fool.

Then Lightning Lil decides to fly.

I am
high up in
the air.

Look at me,
I can loop
the loop!

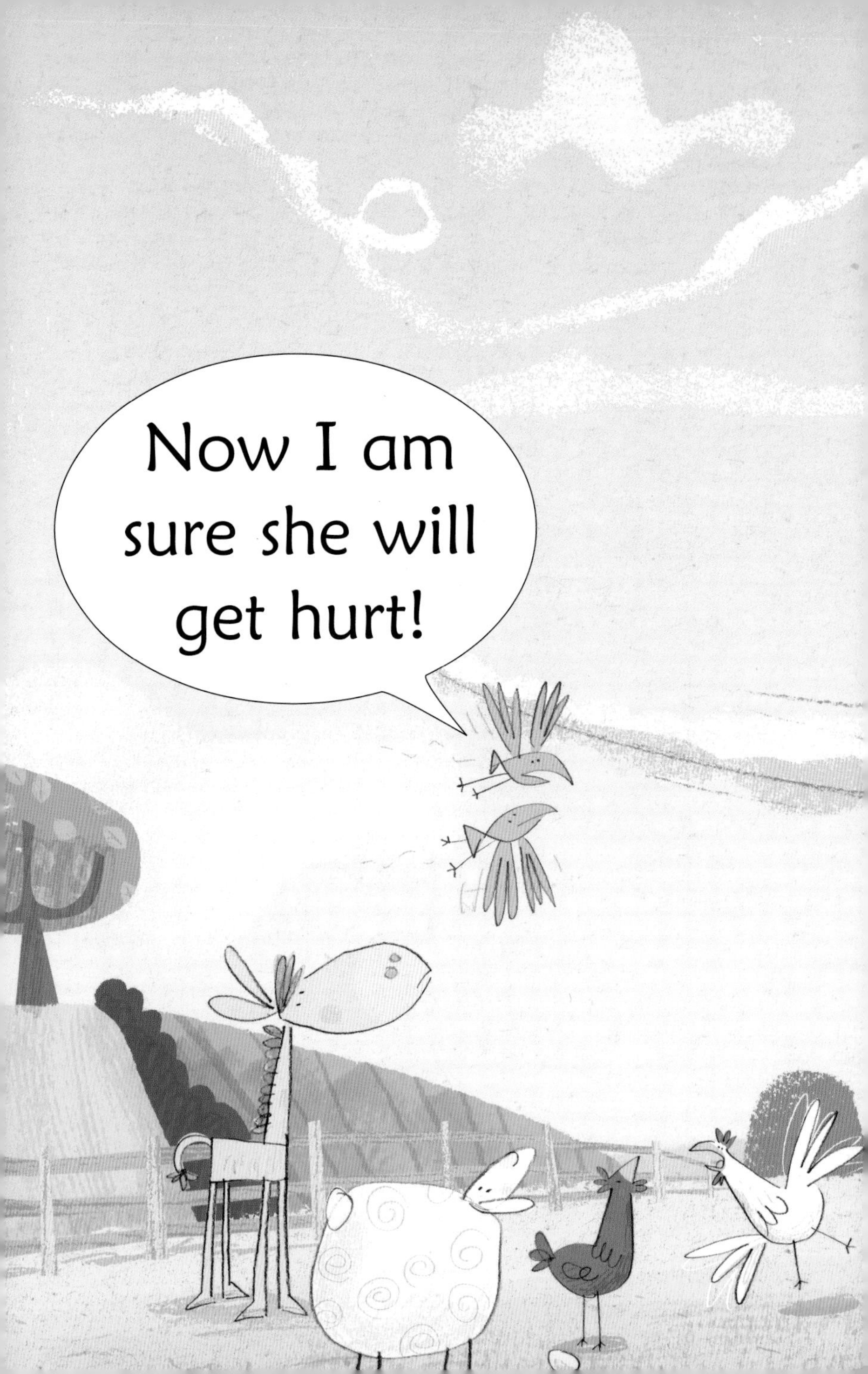
Now I am sure she will get hurt!

But there's more to flying than meets the eye.

It's the quiet life now for Lightning Lil.

Join us back at the farm, dear Lil.

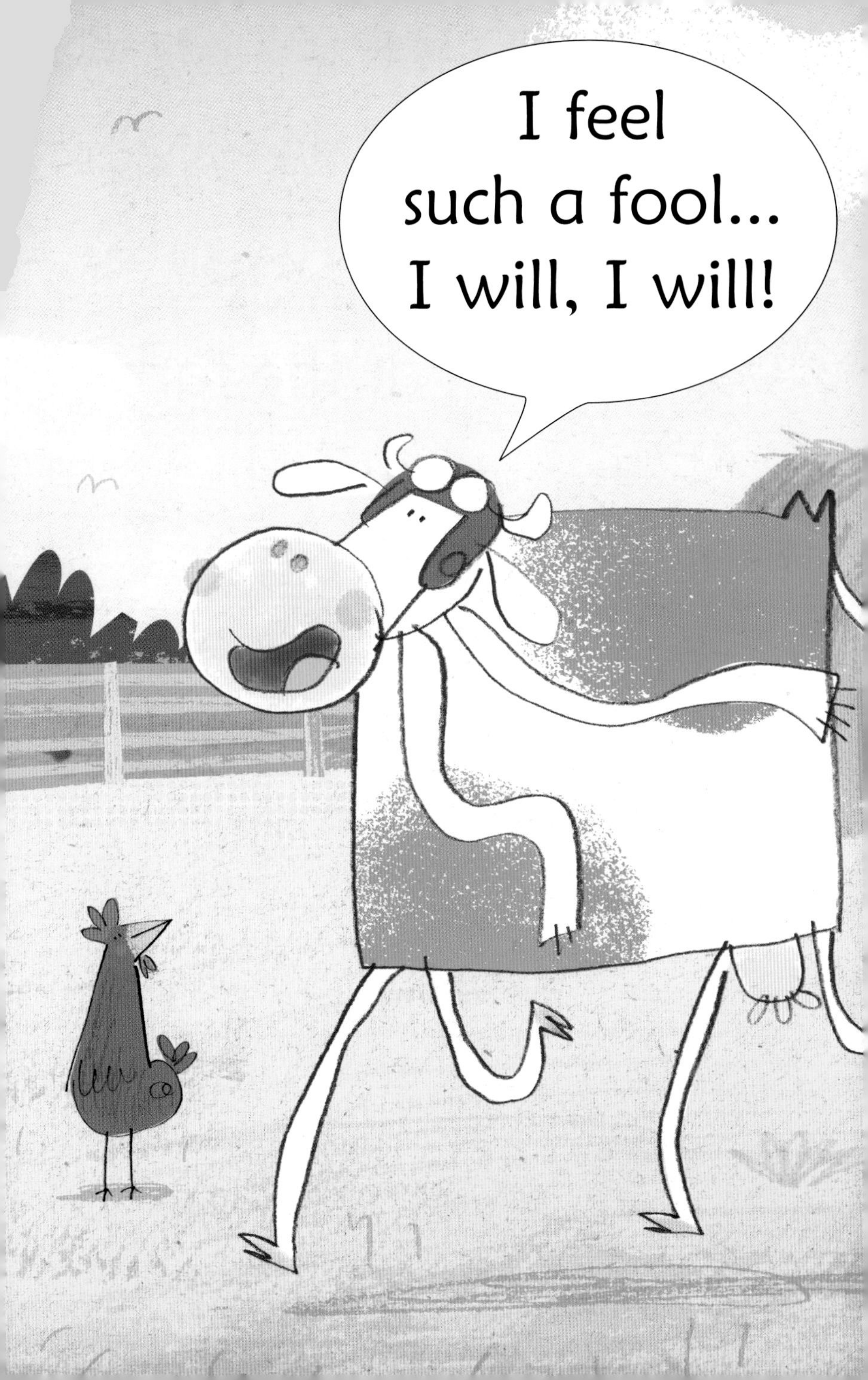
I feel such a fool... I will, I will!

Puzzle 1

Look at the pictures together,
and try retelling the story.

1.

2.

3.

4.

5.

6.

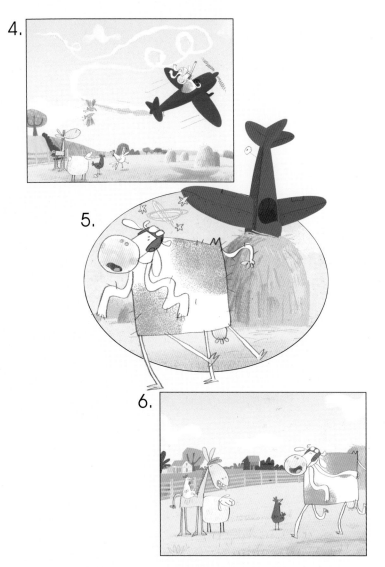

You could have fun talking about what
the other animals would say to Lil after
her adventures.

Puzzle 2

Choose the right word to complete each phrase.

1.

Up and ......

| town | gown | down |

2.

I ...... she will get hurt.

| dear | fear | near |

3.

High up in the ......

fair	chair	air

4.

I am ...... she will get hurt.

cure	pure	sure

Puzzle 3

Look at the pictures, read the sentences, then say whether they are true or false.

1.

Lil has a big red car.

2.

The car is on the road.

3.

Lil can loop the loop.

4.

Lil is up in the air.

Answers to puzzles

Puzzle 1

Use this puzzle to check that your child has understood the story, and have fun discussing what the animals might say.

If your child isn't sure what to say, try asking leading questions such as, "Who's this? What is she doing now?" (Of course, there is more than one possible answer.)

Puzzle 2

1. Up and <u>down</u>.

2. I <u>fear</u> she will get hurt.

3. High up in the <u>air</u>.

4. I am <u>sure</u> she will <u>get</u> hurt.

Puzzle 3

1. True
2. False
3. True
4. False

Guidance notes

Usborne Very First Reading is a series of books, specially developed for children who are learning to read. In the early books in the series, you and your child take turns to read, and your child steadily builds the knowledge and confidence to read alone.

The words for your child to read in **Stop That Cow!** introduce these letter-combinations:

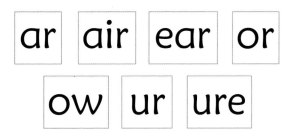

It's well worth giving your child plenty of practice reading these. Later books in the series introduce longer words and new spelling patterns, while reinforcing the ones your child already knows.

You'll find lots more information about the structure of the series, advice on helping your child with reading, extra practice activities and games on the Very First Reading website,* **www.usborne.com/veryfirstreading**

*US readers go to **www.veryfirstreading.com**

Some questions and answers

- **Why do I need to read with my child?**
  Sharing stories and taking turns makes reading an enjoyable and fun activity for children. It also helps them to develop confidence and reading stamina, and to take part in an exciting story using very few words.

- **When is a good time to read?**
  Choose a time when you are both relaxed, but not too tired, and there are no distractions. Only read for as long as your child wants to – you can always try again another day.

- **What if my child gets stuck?**
  Don't simply read the problem word yourself, but prompt your child and try to find the right answer together. Similarly, if your child makes a mistake, go back and look at the word together. Don't forget to give plenty of praise and encouragement.

- **We've finished, now what do we do?**
  It's a good idea to read the story several times to give your child more practice and confidence. Then you can try reading **The Deep Dark Woods** at the same level or, when your child is ready, go on to Book 8 in the series.

Edited by Jenny Tyler and Lesley Sims
Designed by Russell Punter

First published in 2010 by Usborne Publishing Ltd., Usborne House,
83-85 Saffron Hill, London EC1N 8RT, England. www.usborne.com
Copyright © 2010 Usborne Publishing Ltd.